Bear

Porcupine

Worms

Turtle

Rabbit

Hedgehog

Duck

To Ms. Christine—your classroom rules!
—K.G.

To all the teachers—you rule!
—J.F.

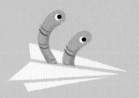

The author would like to thank teacher Nicole Sobieski for her advice and guidance.

Text copyright © 2023 by Kallie George
Cover art and interior illustrations copyright © 2023 by Jay Fleck

Visit us on the Web! rhcbooks.com

Educators and librarians, for a variety of teaching tools, visit us at RHTeachersLibrarians.com

Library of Congress Cataloging-in-Publication Data is available upon request.
ISBN 978-0-593-37878-6 (trade) — ISBN 978-0-593-37879-3 (lib. bdg.) — ISBN 978-0-593-37880-9 (ebook)

The illustrations in this book were created using pencil and digital painting.
The text of this book is set in 25-point Rowboat.
Interior design by Elizabeth Tardiff

MANUFACTURED IN CHINA
10 9 8 7 6 5 4 3 2 1
First Edition

Our Classroom Rules!

by **Kallie George**

illustrated by **Jay Fleck**

RODALE
KiDS

New York

Our classroom rules!
Why?

Read A Book!

Because we try to be on time . . .

What did you eat for breakfast?

A doughnut.

and ready to learn.

and our teacher listens to us.

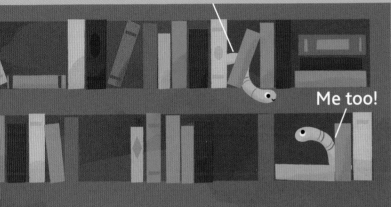

We work by ourselves . . .

and together.

We clean up.

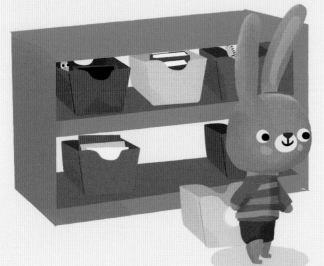

Peekaboo!

Thank you!

We line up.

Let's eat outside.

Yum, I love dirt!

And if we mess up, that's okay.
Mistakes are part of learning.

And we look out for each other.

Ahhhh!

Our classroom rules because . . .

Zzzz . . .

we give new things
a chance.

— Peep!

We share ideas . . .

I can flyyyy!

. . . and express ourselves!

Are you feeling blue?

We take pride in our work.

Worms

Hedgehog

And most of all,
our classroom rules
because we try
to be our best.

Not *the* best. Our best.
Which rules! Just like our classroom.

Bear

Worms

Porcupine

Turtle

Rabbit

Hedgehog

Chick

Duck